Ebenezer Has a Word for Everything

To Joe, Seth, Ethan, Emma, and Claire,
who always believed I could do great things — C. R.

For Victoria — F. D.

Published by
PEACHTREE PUBLISHERS
1700 Chattahoochee Avenue
Atlanta, Georgia 30318-2112
www.peachtree-online.com

Edited by Kathy Landwehr
Design and composition by Nicola Simmonds Carmack
The illustrations were rendered digitally.

Printed in March 2018 by Tien Wah Press, Malaysia
10 9 8 7 6 5 4 3 2 1
First Edition
978-1-56145-848-6
Library of Congress Cataloging-in-Publication Data
Names: Rowe, Chelsea, author. | Dormer, Frank W., illustrator.
Title: Ebenezer has a word for everything / written by Chelsea Rowe ; illustrated by Frank Dormer.
Description: First edition. | Atlanta : Peachtree Publishers, [2018] | Summary: "Ebenezer collects words. No one appreciates his efforts until he
meets a friend who writes stories and could use a word or two." —Provided by publisher.
Identifiers: LCCN 2017017628 | ISBN 9781561458486
Subjects: | CYAC: Vocabulary—Fiction. | Collectors and collecting—Fiction. | Friendship—Fiction.
Classification: LCC PZ7.1.R783 Ebe 2018 | DDC [E]—dc23 LC record available at https://lccn.loc.gov/2017017628

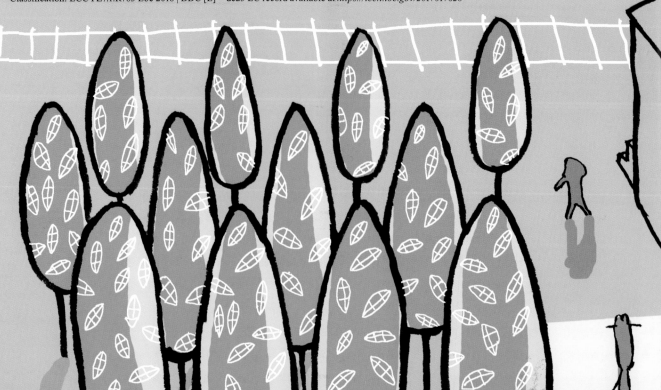

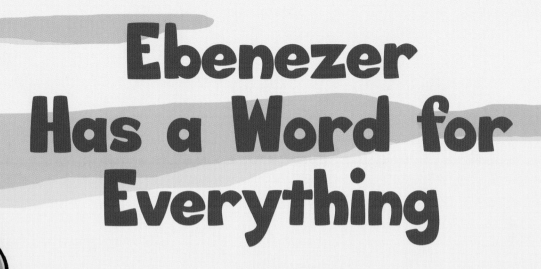

Ebenezer Has a Word for Everything

Written by
Chelsea H. Rowe

Illustrated by
Frank Dormer

Ω
PEACHTREE
ATLANTA

Ebenezer did not collect rocks.

He did not collect stamps.

He did not collect coins.

Ebenezer collected words.

Every day, he discovered new words
to add to his collection.

On the way to school, it was **yield**.

In the grocery store, it was **linguine**.

And on Saturday, it was **possibility**.

Ebenezer kept his collection in his Word Book. It was bright blue with a big *J* on the front.

Why the *J*? Because Ebenezer knew that letters were important too. Without them, there couldn't be any words.

Also, the words for some of his favorite things began with *J*. **Junction**, **juggle**, and **jukebox**, just to name a few.

Ebenezer wanted to share some of the most interesting words in his collection. He had seen lemonade stands before. He figured people needed words more than lemonade.

But it turned out that most people thought they had enough words. They didn't need any new ones.

What a **disappointment**. **Page 2** in his Word Book.

Nevertheless, Ebenezer's Word Book
grew fuller by the day.

"You must have a word for everything,"
his mother said.

He did.

Like the time he saved his allowance to buy
a goldfish.

His mother suggested he name the fish Walter.

His father, Skipper.

His sister, Rainbow.

But Ebenezer knew: there could be no other
name but Arty. Short for **Carassius auratus**.
Right there on **page 32**.

Then there was the day of his sister's
birthday party. The whole house was
filled with shrieking and glitter and pink.

Pink, pink, pink.

Ebenezer hated pink.

It was **exhausting.** Page 21.

And of course, there was also the very worst day ever.

You wouldn't want all the details, but it involved a boring field trip, a missing tuna fish sandwich, a stinky bus, an angry bus driver, and laughing.

Lots of laughing.

Laughing *at* Ebenezer.

There was only one word for a day like that.

Catastrophe. Found on **page 17.**

Ebenezer realized that no one loved words as much as he did.

Sure, his family listened when he told them about **decathalon** over dinner.

And his friends listened when he told them about **parka** on the playground.

And his teacher listened when he told him about **clamor** during class.

SNore!

But questions were the real test of interest.

And no one ever asked him any questions.

Until he met Fitzgerald.

It happened on a Monday. Monday was library day.

Oh, how Ebenezer loved the library! Words everywhere!

He was right in the middle of copying **habitat** into his Word Book when Fitzgerald came over.

"What are you doing?" Fitzgerald asked.

"I'm adding a word to my collection," Ebenezer replied.

"Wow! A word collection! Can I see it?"

That was the day Ebenezer and Fitzgerald became friends.

Now believe it or not, Fitzgerald had a collection
of his own.

"I've got all sorts of ideas," he explained.

"Where?" Ebenezer asked.

"They're all up here," he said, pointing to his head.
"They'd make great stories but I can't make them
sound right. I don't have the right words."

Ebenezer could hardly believe his luck.

He had a word for days like this.

Incredible! Page 5.

Fitzgerald's ideas gave Ebenezer the perfect **opportunity** to put his collection to use.

Ebenezer could think of thirteen words for every one of Fitzgerald's ideas. But he just gave him the top three.

For astronaut ideas, Ebenezer suggested **thermosphere**, **shuttle**, and **solar shield**.

He selected **charlatan**, **impostor**, and **villain** for bad guys.

And **blimey**, **swashbuckler**, and **buccaneer** for pirates.

Together, Ebenezer's words and Fitzgerald's ideas became **sensational** stories.

At recess, Ebenezer and Fitzgerald read their stories aloud, each of them taking a part.

Before you could say **happenstance**, their classmates had gathered around to hear their tales of adventure and mystery and rescue.

Their teacher heard them telling the one about the **ambiguous** alien (who looked surprisingly like Ebenezer's little sister) and asked them to read it for parents' night.

How **embarrassing**. Page 11.

Ebenezer and Fitzgerald went together like *Q* and *U*. Sometimes they were apart but they just made more sense together.

And Ebenezer really did have a word for everything. Including the perfect word for his friendship with Fitzgerald.

It was **stupendous. Page 21.**